The Little Red Hen

A retelling by Violet Findley • Illustrated by Lynne Cravath

Once upon a time, a little red hen decided
to plant some wheat.
"Who will help me plant this?" she asked.

2

"Not me!" said the dog.
"Not me!" said the cat.
"Not me!" said the duck.
You see, they were all quite lazy.

"I will just have to plant it by myself," said the little red hen.

Before long, all the wheat was tall.
"Who will help me cut this?" asked
the little red hen.

"Not me!" said the dog.
"Not me!" said the cat.
"Not me!" said the duck.

"I will just have to cut it by myself," said
the little red hen.

Before long, all the wheat was cut.
"Who will help me grind this?" asked
the little red hen.

"Not me!" said the dog.
"Not me!" said the cat.
"Not me!" said the duck.

"I will just have to grind it by myself," said the little red hen.

Before long, all the wheat was ground.
"Who will help me bake this into bread?"
asked the little red hen.

"Not me!" said the dog.
"Not me!" said the cat.
"Not me!" said the duck.

"I will just have to bake it by myself," said
the little red hen.

Before long, all the bread was baked.
"Who will help me eat this?" asked
the little red hen.

"Me!" said the dog.
"Me!" said the cat.
"Me!" said the duck.

"No! Because you did not help, I will just have to eat this bread by myself," said the little red hen.
And so she did, with jam on top!